The Secret Diary of Julietta Josephine©

10 ½-Step Job Search Guide for Really Smart Girls!

By: Beatrice Louisa Cruz

Illustrated by: Simon Goodway

ISBN-13: 978-0692693216
ISBN-10: 0692693211

For permission requests, write to the publisher, addressed "Attention: Permissions Coordinator," at the address below.

Beatrice Louisa Cruz, LLC
info@beatricelouisacruz.com
www.beatricelouisacruz.com
Tel: 800-757-1506 FREE

It's never too early to instill real-world vocabulary into our young ones. Here's a little book filled with real-life words. Teach now. Instill confidence. Prepare for the grownup world. Here's to our future pilots, chefs, scientists, librarians, mathematicians, professors, engineers, teachers, prime ministers, presidents and everything in between. For all the delightful people Julietta Josephine has met, and for future friendships to come. She's learning, growing, and sharing laughter and love.

- Imagination
- Inspiration
- Motivation
- Courage
- Confidence

Let's never stop instilling these beautiful words into our little ones.

To *J.W.C.B*, with love

10 ½-Step Job Search Guide for Really Smart Girls!

Last summer, my Aunt Vivian invited me to visit her in England. It was my first time out of the United States, and I was incredibly excited! My Aunt Vivian lives in Cambridge where the summer days are long and warm, nights are filled with music and the sounds of laughter from friends chatting with each other. It's also a city notorious for its historical colleges and universities. She took me around several of the campuses and told me one day, I too could attend one if I wanted to. During one of our afternoon adventures, she said she was writing a book on career choices for

women. As we sat sipping tea and eating scones in a lovely, outdoor garden café, she wanted to share her career and job exploration secrets with me so I too would have a career guide when I was ready to find my dream job.

And so the story begins. If you're looking for a new job, or just wanting change from repetition, then look no further than the pages of this life saving book. She's going to give you all the secrets you need to find that ideal career. Believe it or not, that new job is right around the corner. It is normal to be anxious about starting on the long road of job searching, but your journey doesn't have to be hard. It's also extremely important to remember that it's easier to find a job when you already have a job, as the stress of making money is completely removed and you don't end up settling for something that isn't perfect. So if you already have one, hang on to it tightly, while you pursue your new start.

Follow these 10 ½ simple rules and you'll be on the way to landing that dream job in no time:

Rule № 1:

Relax, smile and have fun!
Remember, although these things may seem inconsequential, they are vital! Otherwise, you'll just drive yourself crazy and probably give up on your job hunt. Make time to unwind and de-stress, plant a grin on your face and make sure you have time for excitement. Just don't despair, help is on the way.

Rule № 2:

Network, Network, Network
It can't be stressed enough the power and influence of meeting new people and researching their role within their job and company. When you are dancing at that Friday night party, chatting at casual social gatherings, sharing a burger at a barbeque or looking for the next great read in your local library, etc., you are bound to bump into new, exciting people. It's also always a good idea to let your friends know you are on the lookout for a new job and are eager and motivated to share your skills with others in your area of interest. Who knows, they might have the perfect contact that can point you in the right direction.

Rule № 3:

The all important resume.
  Prepare your resume! Ensure it contains all the pertinent information needed for a prospective employer who is looking for someone just like you. Make it stand out above the rest. It doesn't have to be long; actually, a shorter, more concise resume is usually a lot more effective. Don't let him or her lose you! Make sure you list your name, address, phone number and e-mail address so that a prospective employer is sure to be able to get in contact with you some way or the other. You want to make sure you are reachable when that employer comes a knockin'! You can find a truck load of resume samples on the internet or at your local library if you are lacking inspiration. It's also a good idea to have a friend or family member review it for good measure! You don't want any misspelled words or typos on the document that could hold the key to your future.

Rule № 4:

The Invaluable Informational Interview

Informational Interviews: Taking the leap and going on informational interviews are sometimes a gateway to getting into those hard to reach places. Make a list of people you aspire to meet that work in your field of interest. For example, if you believe working in a dentist's office is for you, or want to be librarian surrounded by books, then get in contact with some! You have nothing to lose and all to gain. When you call, ask them if they would be willing to take a few minutes to meet with you to walk through the journey of their career path. Inform them you've always set your heart on being a librarian, and want to know what it's actually like. Never say you're asking for a 'job' interview; otherwise, they may think you're there looking for a job they don't have available. Instead, inform them you're on an 'information gathering' mission. When you do meet with them, take your resumes with you. It's only at the end of the interview that you'll hand them a resume. This way, you'll have thanked them for their time before asking them to share your resume with their friends or colleagues, who may be looking for someone just like you. If they don't have a job opening at the present time, chances are, someone else will! This is another form of Networking, and it works!

Secret: People love to tell their stories and how they got where they are, it's part of being human, so go for it!

Rule №5:

Dress to Impress
   Preparing for your interview should be as stress-free as ordering a pizza. Wardrobe and jewelry choices should be simple, not too casual; you don't want to look like you have just rolled out of bed and grabbed whatever was on the floor, nor too formal, chances are they are not looking for a ball gown or party dress! Just dress to impress. Young ladies should stick to a suitable black skirt with white blouse, matching jacket and maybe a simple necklace. Remember: you don't get a second chance to make that first impression! Ensure your hair is combed, teeth are brushed, resumes in hand and you're good to go. Arranging to go on informational interviews shouldn't cause you anxiety either, nor should you need to spend tons of money on new clothes. Just ensure you present yourself in a clean and professional manner. And remember to smile!

Rule № 6:

The magic of the *Thank You* note
    After your informational interview, remember to always send a Thank You note. Yes, a real paper Thank You note. You must be thinking: you'll just send an e-mail because it's easier and faster, who sends notes to each other anyway these days. But resist the temptation and it will pay off. Nothing will show your gratitude more than a simple, yet sincere Thank You note. Yes, on real paper!

Rule №7:

Optimize organization

Organize your job search materials and never again will you have to scrabble through weeks worth of mail or trail back months through your browser history. You can buy a notebook with dividers, or find any other folder that works for you. Make sure you remember to write down the person's name, their job title, company and all other vital details. You can even jot down notes before and after your informational interview, you can never have too many notes. Writing down your notes will help you prepare for questions you want to ask before the important meeting. Afterward, you should quickly jot down notes and topics discussed during the meeting. For example, jot down other names or items that might help you in future networking situations.

Rule № 8:

Good Teachers Teach, Great Teachers Inspire!
Talk to your teachers and ask them if they might help you with your job search, usually they will be more than happy to depart their wisdom. If they are genuinely interested in your education and future career opportunities, I'm sure they will point you in the right direction. Remember, they too were in your position once. Chances are, they know of someone who owns a company or needs help with a certain project, and they might recommend you talk to them. It never hurts to talk to as many people as you can. There is nothing to lose. Remember: Network, network, network. That's the golden rule!

Rule № 9:

A Solution in your Pocket
If you can, try to make up some business cards. Most office supply stores sell packages of business cards, and they can be easily made up on home computers. If you don't have the ability of making them yourself at home, a lot of office supply stores print out business cards. There are several different styles you can choose from that won't cost a fortune. Business cards should include your name, address, phone number and e-mail address. These handy cards are a quick and easy tool to have in your pocket when meeting a potential employer. Carry these with you at all times, as you never know when your next network opportunity will arise. On one occasion, my Aunt Vivian gave her card to a classmate of hers in college. Her classmate said they were looking for a translator and the next thing she knew, the company created a position for her and she was hired! So you see, the key is always to be prepared!

Rule №10:

Never Give Up
Repeat! Be motivated enough to go out there and get what you want. Believe and achieve. Jobs are not going to land in your lap, success doesn't come to you, you have to go and grab it. Aunt Vivian says most jobs aren't even advertised in newspapers or on the internet. Why is this I hear you ask? Well, most, if not all employers, would rather hire someone who was referred to them. Sure, a person who has the right skills, interviews well and has a stellar resume may seem the ideal candidate. But by not knowing anything about their personality, how they work in a team, their motivation, that person may not be who the employer thought they were hiring. It pays off to know someone, who knows someone, etc., you get the picture! It is all about who you know.

Rule № 10 1/2:

Don't be afraid of the hard work!
All of the extra energy expended and late nights spent brainstorming and researching pay off, in some way or another. You may inch forward some on a job prospect, or chip away just a tiny bit at some other seemingly insurmountable hurdle, but if you're focused and *working*, your efforts will be rewarded.

If Julietta Josephine has related anything to you, it's that a job seeker has to always be on her game. No social event is JUST a social event; have fun while keeping your mind open to the business opportunities hidden in EVERY interaction, from casual to academic to professional. And since it's also clear that there is no easy, magic formula to an employer finding YOU, keep in mind that *you* have to commit to singing your own praises: be the keeper of your own image and encounters!

Work tirelessly to put yourself in good situations, in front of the right people—and take Julietta Josephine's lead by cultivating and then maintaining an inspired outlook and enthusiasm for this entire thrilling process!

Having been on hundreds of interviews, both informational and employment based, my Aunt Vivian knows first-hand that job hunting and interviewing can be extremely stressful. Remember, the more you practice, the better you'll get at it. You miss 100% of the shots that you don't take. Pretty soon, you'll be so good at it, it'll be second nature and you'll find yourself actually wanting to go on interviews.

The End

About the Author

Beatrice Louisa Cruz was born and raised in a bilingual household in South Texas USA. Her parents are of Mexican-American heritage, and Beatrice Louisa is proud of how her family has stayed close to their language, as well as distinct food, festivals, and other customs. Beatrice Louisa credits extended family—in particular her grandmothers—for shaping who she is today. These strong women taught her to embrace her Mexican heritage and ethnic roots.

School has always been an important focus, and Beatrice Louisa earned a Bachelor's of Science degree in Business Management and International Marketing from Maryville University in St. Louis, Missouri. She went on to secure the Certificate in Public Administration from the Center for Creative Leadership. She now boasts 25-plus years as a Spanish-English translator and a lengthy tenure as procurement professional, working over the years for major aircraft companies and international dignitaries from around the world. Beatrice Louisa is the recipient of numerous awards, enjoying recognition for cost-saving and mentoring initiatives.

Beatrice Louisa 's unique skill set formed via coaching and training roles, especially time spent assisting colleagues on navigating the intricacies of job-searching. She herself has been on both sides of the interview, informational and job-related, and Beatrice Louisa has enjoyed serving on interview panels and on hiring committees.

Beatrice Louisa 's mantra is to help instill confidence today to transform lives for a brighter tomorrow. Her focus on young women around the world means she works with people from all backgrounds and walks of life, acting as a role model, career coach, and mentor to positively reinforce confidence and courage. Beatrice Louisa is committed to shifting the focus off of herself and works with others to help them accumulate the skills and the tools that she knows they can't move forward without.

Beatrice Louisa is uniquely qualified to help a wide population: she is an entrepreneur, artist, musician, businesswoman, and women's advocate who is passionate about others' success. Her own personal and business successes translate into the valuable material that she uses to aid young women, especially those who may not have a role model in their lives, in realizing just how big they can dream, how much they can achieve, and how full their lives and careers may become.

She is eager to use storytelling and fictional characters to bring inspirational messages to life for young women seeking advancement in various fields. Beatrice Louisa 's books feature Julietta Josephine, an appealing character whom young ladies look to for inspirational lessons. The author is hopeful that later in life, a woman might say, "When I was a little girl, I remember *The Secret Diary of Julietta Josephine* and how she found her dream job."

Please visit: www.beatricelouisacruz.com, or e-mail info@beatricelouisacruz.com.

Toll Free: 800-757-1506

Notes:

Notes:

Notes:

Notes:

Notes:

Notes:

Notes:

Notes: